CHANNING O'BANNING
AND THE RAINFOREST RESCUE

ILLUSTRATED BY TAMMIE LYON

BY ANGELA SPADY

NELSON

A Division of Thomas Nelson Publishers

NASHVILLE   DALLAS   MEXICO CITY   RIO DE JANEIRO

Published in Nashville, Tennessee, by Tommy Nelson. Tommy Nelson is an imprint of Thomas Nelson. Thomas Nelson is a registered trademark of HarperCollins Christian Publishing, Inc.

Tommy Nelson titles may be purchased in bulk for educational, business, fund-raising, or sales promotional use. For information, please e-mail SpecialMarkets@ThomasNelson.com.

ISBN-13: 978-0-7180-3262-3

Library of Congress has Cataloged the copyright.

Printed in the United States

15 16 17 18 19 RRD 6 5 4 3 2 1

Mfr: RRD / Crawfordsville, Indiana / April 2015 / PO # 9342852

To C. E. E.
For showing me all of the possibilities with a pencil

Table of Contents

1

Snap Out of It!

Summer vacation was only a few weeks away, but none of my teachers seemed to notice. I was up to my eyeballs in homework. My brain was turning into Jell-O. Even my locker smelled like old cheese. I kept forgetting to take home my lunch box, and green fuzzies were growing on my old sandwich crumbs. School break couldn't get here fast enough!

"Remember, class, there will be a quiz tomorrow," said Mr. Doring, our science teacher. "You *must* know how plants help our environment."

That was the *third* time he'd reminded us today. No wonder we called him Boring Doring. He was about to drive me bonkers. It was like our teacher didn't think we could remember a single thing!

He was the one with Post-it notes all over his desk, after all. He *always* had a bad hair day (that was one thing we had in common) and *always* wore that ginormous red tie with a picture of Einstein saying, "Science is cool" on the front. *Ugh.* My teacher might think science is cool but not me. Why do we have to learn about junk like that?

Art is the only class that I like. After all, I *am* an artist and will be world famous someday. It's only a matter of time before my drawings will be in a museum. I'll probably be forced to wear sunglasses and hide from all my fans. Luckily, I keep a pencil stashed in my ponytail, just in case I need to give an autograph or draw something cool. But for now, I was in science class.

Yuck.

"He must think we're totally clueless," I whispered to Maddy, my best friend.

She didn't move a muscle, so I wasn't sure she'd heard me.

"He's reminded us ten zillion times about that dumb quiz. Why are we having a test this time of the year, anyway?" I said a little louder.

"Uh, right, Chan . . . clueless test . . . a zillion times . . . mmhmm . . ."

Huh? What's her problem?

Every word I'd said had gone in one ear and out the other. Maybe Boring Doring had finally pushed her over the edge. I couldn't blame her.

Maybe she's turned into a science zombie.

I pulled my Lime Lizard Green pencil from my ponytail and dropped it onto the floor on purpose. I needed to check out what Maddy was doing at her desk. If she'd really turned into a zombie, I needed to run for my life.

And then I saw it.

Maddy was in a total daze and writing in her notebook:

MADDY + MARCO 4 EVER

Ugh.

This was all Cooper's fault. Wait—no, it was really all Marco Ramos' fault!

Marco was the new kid at school. Well, he wasn't *that* new. He'd been here for almost a month and seemed like any other fourth grade boy to me. We didn't know much about him, only that he spoke Spanish and English, which was cool, I guess, and that his dad was looking for a new job.

But yesterday Marco told Cooper that he thought Maddy was cute, and, of course, Cooper had to run straight to tell Maddy. Cooper Newberry is one of my best friends, but he blabs everything to the entire planet. And now, thanks to the big mouth, Maddy has gone goofy in science class—all because of a boy.

"Helllloooo, earth to Maddy, come in for a landing . . . do you hear meeee?" I snapped my fingers as loudly as possible, trying to get her attention.

Just when Maddy noticed I was alive, I felt our teacher standing right behind my desk. His stare was burning a hole into my ponytail.

"Miss Channing O'Banning, do you have something you'd like to tell the class?" Mr. Boring glared over the top of his glasses, like one of those mad scientists on the sci-fi channel.

"Uh, no . . . um . . . sorry, Mr. Boring," I said quickly.

The whole class cracked up.

"Oh! I mean Mr. Doring—*not* Mr. Boring . . . sir!" I corrected myself.

Cooper laughed so hard that I thought his head might blow off. His whole face turned red. Almost purple, really. *It wasn't that funny.*

But just when I was about to get the Boring Doring lecture on "No Talking While the Teacher Is Talking," the bell rang for class to be over. *Yes!* I couldn't leave science class fast enough.

"Way to go, Chan," Cooper griped. "The last

thing we need is for Boring Doring to get mad at everyone during the last week of school. He could really make this test a doozy."

Secretly, I wanted to yell at Cooper for blabbing to Maddy that Marco said she was cute. That's what started this whole thing in the first place. But I couldn't get too mad. Cooper had been one of my best friends since kindergarten. He understood me better than anyone. Maddy understood me too, but now she was in Marco La La Land.

"I don't see *why* we have to know so much about a bunch of dumb plants," I complained.

"I don't think Mr. Doring cares what you think, Chan. And we still have to take the quiz. Otherwise, we'll flunk and have to take the class again next year."

Cooper did have a point. I couldn't face the future if Boring Doring were in my life for two years in a row. Cooper always thinks of things ahead of time, which is exactly why he is the smartest kid in class. He remembers to study for every single quiz, and he always remembers to complete every assignment. Basically, Cooper is exactly the opposite of me. I tried not to think about things that stunk. And to me, science is one of the stinkiest things *ever*. Cooper Newberry loves it.

"I'll help you guys study for the quiz," said

someone behind us. "I know a lot about plants and animals and stuff."

That's when I looked over my shoulder. *Ugh.* It was You-Know-Who.

Apparently, Marco liked stinky science too. Of course.

Marco and Maddy were walking right behind us. I couldn't help but glance over at Cooper. He didn't seem to be as bugged about it as I was.

"Oh, yeah?" I asked Marco. "Are you a plant and animal expert or something?"

I didn't need anyone's help—especially from Marco, the Best Friend Thief.

"We learned about all kinds of plants at my old school in Costa Rica. There's every plant you can imagine in the rainforest. In fact, some of the plants and animals don't exist anywhere else in the world."

I looked over at Maddy, and she was grinning from ear to ear. She looked at Marco like he was some kind of genius. I couldn't help but roll my eyes.

I wanted to scream.

"We have zoos around here, you know," I pointed out. "*And* planetariums."

"Uh, Chan, planetariums study *planets*, not plants," Cooper whispered.

Oh, whatever!

"You may know something about plants, Marco, but I happen to know *everything* about animals," I said.

That was one thing I was sure about. After all, I could draw *any* and *every* kind of animal. I looked over at Cooper, hoping he'd agree that I was an animal expert. I finally had to poke him with my elbow to make sure he got the hint.

"Ow! Yeah, Chan knows *tons* about animals and stuff," Cooper said.

I thought Maddy might speak up and agree with Cooper, but no such luck. I doubt that she even knew I was standing there.

"Have *you* ever seen a blue jeans frog, Channing O'Banning?" Marco asked. "Or a quetzal bird? They're very hard to spot in the wild since their tail looks like a long green fern."

A blue jeans frog? And what *kind of bird did he say?*

I couldn't help but laugh. So did Cooper. Marco must have thought we'd believe anything. I couldn't even pronounce the type of bird he had mentioned. It sounded like the word *pretzel* to me. And no wonder they're hard to spot—I'm sure they don't even exist!

"Yeah, right!" I said. "I guess you've seen purple elephants or giraffes that wear sneakers too, huh?"

Everyone laughed at my comeback—everyone except Marco and Maddy, of course.

"Whatever, Channing O'Banning. Come on, Maddy, let's get to class. Some people are just rude."

Maddy zoomed around Cooper and me with her nose stuck up in the air. If the sprinkler system had gone off, she would have drowned. My *ex*-best friend walked around with Mr. Plant Expert, acting like we didn't exist.

Oh, why did that boy have to move to Greenville?!

I couldn't wait to go home and get out my Candy Apple Red pencil and my secret sketchbook. I already knew what I was going to draw: a picture of Maddy with a big red X over her face.

Best friends—who needs them?

2

BFF

I remember the very first time I met my best friend Madison Martinez. Our preschool teacher had put our desks in alphabetical order. Since *Martinez* came before *O'Banning*, Maddy sat right in front of me. She had the curliest brown hair I'd ever seen. And Maddy said she'd never seen a kid with as many freckles as I had. She asked if anyone had ever tried to connect the dots on my arms and legs. I tried that later with a purple marker and got in big trouble.

Once in preschool, when I was really bored, I slid a jumbo crayon into a curl on the back of Maddy's head. She didn't even notice it until Cooper blabbed about it. I thought it looked good with her pink outfit, but Maddy didn't think so. She tattled on me to the teacher in two seconds. I had to stay in at recess and everything.

I drew a picture of a pink giraffe and told Maddy that I was really sorry. We've been best friends ever since—or *had* been best friends—until Marco Ramos came along.

Maddy and I always had fun at sleepovers too. She took ballet lessons and would try to teach me a few of her moves. In exchange, I'd give Maddy a few drawing lessons and let her use my colored pencils. We soon decided to stick to what we liked best, though. My legs felt like pretzels when I tried standing in one of those ballet positions. And Maddy couldn't even draw a turtle, which seemed like the easiest thing in the world to me.

Sometimes we'd have a sleepover at my Nana O'Banning's house. She's the coolest grandmother on the planet, and Maddy thinks so too. Maddy once brought over some old dance costumes from her ballet recitals so we could play dress up. We even dressed up Teeny, my Nana's pot-bellied pig, in a pink tutu. He didn't seem to mind at all. Actually, I think he kind of liked it. Teeny twirled and twisted around like he was on a real stage. Nana even gave him a rose, but I can't remember if he smelled it or ate it.

But I looked weirder than Teeny. I felt silly in the pink tights and purple leotard that Maddy had picked out for me. She even took the pencil out of my ponytail and crammed a sparkly princess crown on my head. And the ballet shoes were horrible! They cramped my toes so badly that I could hardly walk. It took two whole days to straighten out my feet enough to wear my high-top sneakers again.

Maddy was a natural ballerina. She could do leaps and stand on her tiptoes like it was the easiest thing in the world. She was the best dancer in the whole school.

It was going to be weird not having Maddy as one of my best friends. She probably wouldn't miss me at all.

That dumb Marco had messed up everything!

After getting home from school and gobbling down a few gummy turtles, I tried not to think about Maddy. I had other stuff to worry about—like a dumb plant quiz!

But for some reason, my brain was asleep. I couldn't concentrate on a single thing. Instead, I doodled all over my science papers. I knew all of that plant stuff anyway. A flower grows from a seed. The seed needs water and sunlight. Bees get the pollen and take it to other plants. *Blah, blah, blah.*

I think Boring Doring was trying to make us all drop out of fourth grade. If only he'd remember that everyone wasn't as excited about science as he was—everyone except Marco. I still didn't get why he had to act like the world's greatest expert on plants and animals. *Grrr . . .*

And Marco didn't just go on and on about science stuff—he also told everyone he played soccer and had been on the starting team at his old school. I mean, really, who cares?

Maddy, that's who.

In gym class, I overheard her ask Marco, "Will you teach me how to play soccer? I don't know a single thing about that sport! I'd just *love* to learn."

You have got to be kidding me!

"Since when do you like sports?" I couldn't help but ask. "Who *are* you, Maddy? What has happened to you?"

But my ex-best friend looked at me like I was a total dimwit. "What's wrong with wanting to try something new, Chan? Maybe you'd like it too— that is, if you weren't always so rude to Marco!"

Ugh!

I slammed my locker, and Maddy slammed hers right back. It was awful. I ran to the bathroom as quickly as possible. I didn't want anyone—especially Maddy—to see that I was about to burst into tears. If only Marco Ramos could go right back to where he had come from!

3

Beware of Frogs Wearing Sneakers

Strawberry gummy turtles are the yummiest snack ever, and I can't get enough of them. I keep them in my backpack, on my bookshelf, and in all the pockets of my jeans. My big sister, Katie, thinks that gummies fry my brain, but what does she know? I will admit that every time I eat them before bed, I *do* have the craziest dreams.

For example, last night I dreamed that Marco was the star of a TV show about the jungle. He even wore a tan shirt and shorts like all those other zoo people. He swung through the trees with a monkey on his shoulder and fought a monster plant with giant arms and legs. I was in the dream, too, and about to be eaten by a strange red frog wearing blue jeans. It even wore a pair of my high-top sneakers! Just when I was about to become its lunch, I screamed out loud and woke up Katie.

"Hey, loud mouth!" she yelled from across the hallway. "*Some* people are trying to sleep around here! Did you forget it's Saturday morning? *Geez!*"

I was so glad to be awake and out of that *awful* nightmare that I didn't even care Katie was so grouchy. I rubbed my eyes to snap out of it and tried to go back to sleep, but it was no use. The only thing I saw when I closed my eyes was that crazy monster plant.

I had to think of something else. Maybe if I studied about normal-size plants, I might get bored and fall asleep.

But that was no help either.

I got out my sketchbook and drew the ginormous

plant from my dream. Sometimes when I draw something that scares me, it helps get it out of my head. I slowly drew the giant green leaves, an orange center, and wavy purple petals. Then I picked out a pencil called Puppy Nose Pink. It was the exact color of my skin, minus all the freckles. I drew the arms and legs next, added scary-looking eyes, and sketched a mouthful of teeth. It had to be Marco's fault that I'd had such a crazy nightmare in the first place. After all, he was the one who'd been going on and on about imaginary animals.

Suddenly, Katie barged into my room before I had a chance to hide my sketchbook.

"Ever heard of knocking?" I asked Katie, the Snoop. *Why is she bugging me?*

"Ever heard of *not* screaming in your sleep?" she asked. "I think you woke up everyone on Darcy Street. You're just lucky I was able to go back to sleep, or you would have been sorry. It was just a dream, you big baby."

"Duh," I said and went back to my drawing. Maybe if I just ignored her, she'd go away.

"Wow. What's with the freaky drawing you've got there?" Katie asked, glancing over at my sketchbook.

"Oh, it's nothing." I flipped over my drawing so she wouldn't stare.

"Nothing, bluffing! Since when did you start drawing weird stuff like that?" she asked.

"What are you, a detective?" I was tired of Katie asking so many questions.

"Whatever," she said, flopping down onto my beanbag chair without asking. "I heard your class got a new kid from Mexico or something. Maybe you can brush up on those Spanish words that Mom makes us practice. What does he look like? Is he cute?"

"That does it! Get *out* of my room, Katie! I'm tired of your crazy questions. And he's from Costa Rica— not Mexico. And I don't care what he looks like, or what he does, or anything!"

"Okay, okay . . . touchy, touchy!" said Katie, rolling her eyes. "I think I'm on to something, huh?" She smiled like she knew some big secret.

I pushed Katie out of my room and locked the door.

I'd had it with the Snoop, and I was tired of talking about Marco Ramos. If I heard one more word about the new kid, I thought I might explode into a zillion pieces. All I wanted to do was relax on a Saturday morning and watch TV.

I pulled on my fuzzy robe and put my hair up into a ponytail. It had a zillion lumps and stray hairs sticking out, but I didn't care. It looked better once I stuck my Pookie Purple pencil in the top.

I could smell Mom's chocolate chip pancakes from upstairs and could almost taste their gooey goodness. Since Mom loved sleeping in on Saturdays too, she rarely made pancakes unless it was a special occasion. But it wasn't anyone's birthday or Mom and Dad's anniversary. I slid down the stair rail and bumped into Dad, splattering his coffee a little. *Oops.*

"Well, good morning to you too," he said. "Did you sleep well?"

"Not really," I yawned. "I sort of had a bad dream last night."

"Uh-oh, that's too bad. Want to talk about it?"

"No, I'm okay. It was just a dumb dream. No big deal," I sort of fibbed. "Those chocolate chip pancakes smell delicious!"

"As soon as Katie comes downstairs, your mom and I will share a super-special announcement!"

Weird. Very weird. What are they up to?

All I could think about was spreading butter on my pancakes and drowning them in yummy syrup. I was one bite away from sweet chocolate heaven.

Katie finally made it to the kitchen. If only Mom and Dad would hurry up with their news—my stomach was doing backflips.

"Dear, would you like to tell the girls, or should I?" asked Mom, smiling from ear to ear.

What's with them? Have they been eating my school glue?

"Does everyone remember how hard I've been trying to find more help at the clinic?" asked Dad. "Things have gotten really busy, and I could use another doctor to help out. Well, yesterday was the day! I finally found someone."

Is that the big news? Boring!

I mean, I was glad Dad found some help, but I had more important things to worry about—like chocolate chip pancakes! I crammed the biggest bite ever into my mouth.

"Dr. Ramos is a nice doctor who just moved to Greenville. I think he'll be a great addition to the clinic."

I choked on my pancake and spit it out onto my plate.

Ramos?! That was Marco's last name.

It can't be. It just can't be!

"Hey, that's great news, Dad! I bet he's from Costa Rica, isn't he?" asked Katie, sneakily smiling at me.

"Why, yes, Katie. Yes, he is. And, Chan, I think his son is in your class. His name is Marlon . . . or Mark?"

I felt dizzy. This was not happening.

"It's Marco. Marco Ramos, Dad," I gulped. I wanted to wipe that smile right off Katie's face.

"Yes, that's it! You two will become great friends. I think we should invite them over for dinner tomorrow. We'll introduce ourselves a little more."

This is not happening.

"That's a great idea, dear! I'll call Mrs. Ramos today," Mom chimed in.

This wasn't another silly dream.

It was a real nightmare!

4

D for Doomed!

Dinner with the Ramos family went better than I expected. Our parents talked about boring stuff, and Katie kept waiting for me to say something stupid. Mom fixed spaghetti, so I stared at the meatballs instead of looking at Marco. He hardly spoke a word, which was fine by me. Maybe Marco had figured out that I knew more about animals than he ever would.

Thanks to my quick thinking, I told Mom that I had a stomachache and needed to go to my room. But I actually did have studying to do. I was going to ace Boring Doring's science quiz. That would show Mr. Plant Genius!

On Monday morning, Boring Doring could hardly wait to pass out the big quiz. It was almost like he wanted us to flunk! I read each question over and over, hoping the answers would pop into my brain. My hands were so sweaty that I could hardly hold my pencil. The quiz was *horrible*! The words just swam around on the page, and I don't think I answered a single question correctly.

I was the last one to turn in my paper.

"That quiz *stunk*!" said Cooper. "The drawing of those plant parts looked nothing like the one in our book. What did you think about it, Chan?"

Cooper freaked out about every single test, which made no sense to me. Everyone knew that he was a brainiac and made a big fat A on everything. Since A's never happened to me, sometimes Cooper's freak-outs really bugged me.

"I'm not too worried about it," I fibbed. I didn't want to hear Cooper blab on about it if I didn't have to. "It was a piece of cake."

My head was still spinning from trying to think up all the answers. I could feel my heart beating between my ears.

"What did you think about the quiz, Marco?" Cooper asked.

Oh, why do we need his opinion on things?

"It wasn't too bad," said Marco. "My mom made me study extra hard. I even practiced labeling a drawing of a plant at home, just to make sure that I could do it."

Of course he did.

"I guess we'll find out soon enough," said Cooper. "Boring Doring's grading them during recess."

I'd have been happier if our teacher would have waited for a few days. Or maybe for a week. Or for an eternity.

"How do you think you did, Chan?" asked Maddy.

I was shocked that my ex-best friend was even talking to me. In the last few days, Maddy and I had hardly spoken a word to each other. She probably just wanted another excuse to talk about how smart Marco was.

Grrr . . .

Just as I was about to turn my back to ignore Maddy, the bell rang for class to start. Boring Doring stood up front with a huge smirk on his face. He had our graded papers in his hands, and I could tell I was totally right—he *did* want us to fail. *Gulp.*

This could be bad. This could be really, *really* bad. Maybe I should ask to be excused and hide out in the bathroom. It would be just my luck that the school nurse would find me, and she'd call Dad.

Then I'd be forced to take medicine that tasted like sewer water. No, thank you.

Boring Doring walked up and down the rows of desks, handing back our papers. He usually wrote our scores at the top with a giant red marker. He wrote it so big that everyone in the entire room could see it. They could probably see it from Mars.

My mouth was so dry that I could barely swallow. I felt like I'd eaten an entire jar of peanut butter. Luckily, Boring Doring wrote our scores with a pencil this time. Otherwise, everyone in class would have seen the giant D on my paper.

I am doomed! I'm going to be dead meat when I get home.

Maybe if I'd studied a little more instead of drawing in my sketchbook, I would have gotten a better grade.

But wait . . .

It's all Marco's fault . . . right?

If he hadn't told Cooper that he thought Maddy was cute, Maddy wouldn't be acting so crazy. *I* wouldn't have lost my best friend over a dumb boy; *I* wouldn't have gotten upset; *I* wouldn't have had a bad dream; and *I* wouldn't have drawn in my sketchbook instead of studying for that dumb quiz.

It *was* all Marco's fault.

Oh, and to make matters a *zillion* times worse,

while I was daydreaming about being grounded for all eternity, I didn't notice that my quiz paper had slid off my desk, floated through the air, and landed directly under Marco's desk.

It was like the whole thing happened in slow motion, and there was nothing I could do about it. It was horrible!

"For a girl who acts like a know-it-all, it sure doesn't look like it on this quiz," Marco smarted, looking at my paper.

How dare he!

I quickly snatched my paper out of his hands and crammed it into my book bag. I also noticed that Maddy had seen the *whole* thing. Thank goodness she didn't see my score, thanks to my quick action. But I *knew* she overheard Marco acting rude toward me. She didn't say a single word to back me up or defend me. She just sat there . . . like a statue . . . like an *ex*-best friend . . . and did *nothing*.

But when Marco showed her his grade, she went crazy. "Wow, you are so *smart*, Marco. I'll bet your A+ is the highest score in the class!"

Ugh.

Summer vacation, get me out of here!

5

We're Doing What?

Before Marco messed up everything, Maddy and I would walk to the bakery every Wednesday and get a cherry-vanilla cupcake.

But I left school without even looking for Maddy—I was not speaking to her after what happened in science class. Even though I still walked by the bakery, I just couldn't go in. It wasn't the same without my best friend.

Instead, I went home and ate the next-best thing: a grilled cheese stuffed with pickles and potato chips. Nana O'Banning had shown me how to make it all by myself because it was her favorite too. She and Teeny were coming over for dinner, and I couldn't wait to see the most adorable pig on earth. Maybe he'd cheer me up a little.

———

"Hey, gang, time for dinner!" yelled Dad. "It's a special meal for some special news!"

What could he be up to this time?

"I don't even want to guess about this one," I told Katie as we came downstairs. "The last time Dad had a surprise, it was about Dr. Ramos working at the clinic. This better not have anything to do with Marco."

"Are you still upset with him? He's cool, Chan," said Katie. "You're just jealous that he likes Maddy Martinez."

"I am not! You don't know *anything*!"

Katie could be such a pain.

"Are you girls coming, or is all this food for Teeny and me?" asked someone from the kitchen. I'd know that voice anywhere.

"Hey, Nana! Hi, Teeny!" I said, running to give them both hugs. "Do you know what Dad's news is all about? Can you give me a hint?"

Nana winked and then tugged at my ponytail. "He mentioned that it has something to do with summer vacation. I guess it will be a surprise for all of us!"

Anything about summer vacation *was* good news. Maybe we were going to the beach. Or maybe New York City! I could visit tons of art museums there. Teeny and I sat at the table and tried to be patient. We were both starving. I even heard Teeny's stomach growl. Or maybe it was mine.

But when Mom brought food to the table, I didn't recognize anything.

Weird. Very weird.

"I hope I fixed the recipes correctly," said Mom. "Mrs. Ramos gave them to me. It's what they eat in Costa Rica!"

Not again.

"The chicken dish is *arroz con pollo*, which means 'rice with chicken.' It comes with black beans too. Everyone has to try it," Mom insisted.

She'd also fixed something that looked like cooked bananas, which were still hot.

Cooked bananas? Has she gone off her rocker?

I'd rather eat school cafeteria food.

"These are plantains, Channing," Mom said. "They're sort of like bananas, only better. At least try one. You know the rule."

Katie and I had to try at least one bite of anything new. Sometimes Mom's rule really stunk. Like *now*. I looked around to make sure that a trash can was close by. I held my nose and took a bite of the chicken. It was spicy . . . but *delish*!

I took a deep breath before trying the banana-plantain thingies. This could be gross. This could be really, *really* gross.

Bananas are already slimy enough as it is, right?

But I put the tiniest bite possible on my fork and touched my tongue to it. Then I took a teensy, weensy bite . . .

Yum! Who knew that weird banana things could be so tasty?

Teeny decided to brave it out too. Nana filled his bowl with the Costa Rican food, and he went bonkers! I'd never seen his hairy little ears flap so fast. He buried his head so far into the bowl that all I could see was his tail.

"Look at that pig go!" Nana said, chomping on a plantain. "If all the food in Costa Rica tastes this good, then I'm ready to go there someday!"

"I agree with Nana," said Katie. "I can't believe that I'm saying this, but I like this stuff!"

"It's all in the spices," confessed Mom. "Mrs. Ramos brought those over too."

How come everyone in the Ramos family was so nice except Marco? I just didn't understand it.

"That brings me to the big news," said Dad. "Your mom and I have decided where we're all going for summer vacation."

Yes!

Katie and I held hands and crossed our fingers under the table.

"Just as long as there's a shopping mall," Katie whispered to me.

"And a craft store with pencils," I whispered back.

"As you know, one of the reasons I hired Dr. Ramos is so I can take some time off and do things with the family. And this summer, we'll finally get the chance to go on a fantastic vacation," Dad announced.

I could hardly wait. I even crossed my toes for extra luck.

"Dr. Ramos has invited us to stay at his house in Costa Rica. We'll tour the whole country!"

I'd never seen Dad so excited.

That makes one of us.

"Yay!" Mom and Nana squealed, giving each other high fives. Teeny squealed too, even though I knew he didn't have a clue where Costa Rica was on a map. Come to think of it, neither did I.

I was too shocked to say anything.

What in the world is in Costa Rica?

Why couldn't we go somewhere fun, like other normal kids? What was Dad thinking? And I *sure* didn't want to stay in Marco's house!

No way, no how, not in a gazillion years!

I must've looked like I had swallowed a thousand lemons because Dad picked up on my sour mood immediately.

"What's wrong, Chan?" asked Dad. "Aren't you excited? You'll get to see lots of wild animals and butterflies. Who knows, we may even get a chance to zip line. You know, ride through the trees on a long wire? You'd love that, wouldn't you?"

Acting like Tarzan of the Jungle didn't sound very fun to me. But Dad did mention wild animals and butterflies . . . It would be fun to draw those. At least I would be miles and miles away from Marco and Maddy.

Costa Rica might be more fun that I'd thought. Maybe I'll get a tiny bit excited.

"One more thing, Chan," Mom said. "We're also going to take Marco Ramos with us. His parents are nice enough to let him go along. Marco will show us around his home and help us with our Spanish."

What in the world?

Katie let out a big laugh. I kicked her under the table with both feet.

What are my parents thinking?! There was no way that I was going out of the country, out of town, or even down the street with Marco Ramos!

This cannot be happening! Maybe I'll run away and join the circus. Surely someone could use an artist.

"Nana, can I spend the night with you and Teeny?" I asked nicely, hoping she'd say yes. My grandmother knew me better than anyone, and she could tell I was upset about the news. But I knew better than to tell my parents there was absolutely no way I was going anywhere with Mr. Know-It-All Marco.

"That's a great idea, Chan. I think it's time we have some fun in the Secret Artist Hangout."

6

Salad Surprise

It felt good to be back at the Secret Artist Hangout. That was what Nana and I liked to call my bedroom at her house. From my snuggly stuffed animals to the yellow stars on the ceiling, it was the perfect room in every way.

I was so upset over Dad's news that all I wanted

to do was get out my sketchbook and draw. It always made me feel better. I pulled my Chocolate Brownie Brown pencil from my ponytail and drew a girl with curly hair and a pink bow.

"Mind if I come in, Chan?" asked Nana. "Would you like to talk a little? You draw, and I'll listen. How does that sound?"

Nana O'Banning always knew just what to say. I kept drawing and got out some of my other pencils.

"I don't understand why you're not tickled pink about going to Costa Rica. Your dad said we could even bring Teeny along. I'm as excited as Teeny is in a yard full of mud puddles!"

I smiled a little and kept drawing.

"I may be wrong, but it looks like you're drawing a picture of Maddy," Nana said. "How is she? I haven't seen her around lately."

I wasn't sure if I felt like talking about Maddy, but I knew talking to Nana might make me feel better. "We're sort of not best friends anymore. All she worries about is Marco, Marco, Marco. It stinks!"

Nana picked up a pencil and began drawing with me.

"Is that it? I'm sure she still wants you as her best friend, Chan. Just because things don't always go your way doesn't mean that Maddy isn't your friend. Remember what it says in Proverbs—a friend loves at *all* times. Maddy might be friends with Marco, but it's okay to be friends with lots of people."

It didn't sound okay to me. It sounded like the worst idea ever.

"I don't know, Nana. I'll have to think about it. Maybe I should quit being mad . . . *maybe*."

"That's my girl. I'm sure that she's just as upset as you are and misses you too," Nana pointed out.

"I doubt it. Maddy's probably forgotten even my name or where I live."

"Oh, fiddle faddle! The best thing to do is talk to her about it at school," Nana said. "And if you don't mind me saying, you need to be nice to Marco too."

Ugh. That is pushing it.

I looked down at the letters that Nana had written at the bottom of my paper:

CHANNING + MADDY = BEST FRIENDS FOREVER

It was finally the last week of school.

I needed every bonus point I could get in science class. I couldn't watch TV for a whole week because I'd bombed the last quiz. Dad even threatened to take my pencils away for a month. That was enough to snap me back to reality.

Boring Doring put us in teams for our last project. This time he put Maddy and me together. She didn't look too happy about it, and I got a little nervous. But I kept thinking about what Nana had said at the Secret Artist Hangout.

"Class, since we're studying about plants this week, we're going to make a giant salad and study all of its parts," said Boring Doring. "Not only will it be a healthy snack, but you'll learn something too!"

Weird. Very weird.

"I'll give each team a vegetable that's cut into two pieces. Look at it closely, and then draw its insides in your notebook."

Mr. Doring was the only one who looked excited.

"This is one strange assignment, don't you think, Maddy?" I asked nervously.

Maddy seemed shocked that I even spoke to her. She sort of smiled back.

"Who knows, Chan? But he's coming over to our table now," she whispered. "I think we're getting the cucumber. He gave Cooper and Marco a squishy tomato. Gross!"

Does she have to bring up Marco's name again?

"Yeah . . . gross," I mumbled. I thought about

offering to draw a picture of the cucumber and the seeds for our project but changed my mind. Maddy would probably inform me that Marco was a better artist than I am too. I wasn't about to take any chances.

"By the way, I don't have a crush on Marco anymore, but we're still friends."

"Why didn't you tell me?" I asked, shocked by the news.

"Because you never asked," said Maddy. "You only hung out with Cooper and totally ignored me."

"What? Uh, no, that isn't true, Maddy," I corrected her. "You wanted to hang out with Marco and acted like I was invisible!"

"Whatever," Maddy said, rolling her eyes.

"Yeah, whatever!" I said, crossing my arms and turning my back to her. But I couldn't help but think of what Nana had told me at the Secret Artist Hangout. *Maybe I should give Maddy a chance . . .*

"Since we're admitting stuff, I got a big fat D on the science quiz last week," I turned around and confessed. Maybe Maddy would feel sorry for me.

"Wow," said my ex-BFF. "Too bad for you."

I didn't think Maddy felt sorry for me one bit! So much for giving her a chance. I'm sure she and Mr. Science Genius would laugh together about how I almost flunked the quiz. It would probably be all over fourth grade by the end of the day.

But what if Nana were right? What if Maddy and I could be best friends again someday? That was one big *if.*

Having Maddy Martinez as my BFF wasn't about to happen anytime soon.

7

Asombroso!

"School's out, school's out, Teeny has a great big snout!"

Nana loved singing anytime we were about to go on vacation. And since we were traveling all the way to Costa Rica, I made sure to pack my headphones. That would also give me an excuse to ignore Marco. If I couldn't hear him, then I didn't have to talk to him. *Yes!*

After taking our seats on the plane, Nana reached into her big purse. I hoped she'd packed a bag of gummy turtles.

"Before we take off, I thought you might need a new pencil to take to Costa Rica. This one will even match your high-top sneakers, Chan."

Nana handed me a pencil with a strange name: Blue Morpho. I wasn't sure what the name meant, but I couldn't wait to use it. It matched perfectly with my blue polka-dot sneakers.

"Thanks, Nana! I'll be sure to draw something cool for you and Teeny. Who knows? Maybe I'll even draw something for Cooper . . . and maybe Maddy. Maybe."

I didn't tell her that Marco was still mad at me for making fun of him at school. I'm sure making up crazy names like *blue jeans frog* and *quetzal bird* was just his way of trying to be funny and fit in. But there was no way he was telling the truth, and that really bugged me! Lying is wrong, and so in my book, Marco was wrong too. He only talked to Teeny and Katie during the whole plane ride, which was fine by me.

I was ready to get off the plane and go back to Greenville. Teeny didn't like being on the plane either. He kept opening and closing his mouth so that his ears would pop. My ears hurt too, and we even split a stick of gum, hoping that would help. But Teeny blew a bubble bigger than his whole head, and then the bubble burst. It took forever to peel the gum out of his ears.

Once we landed in Costa Rica, Marco helped us hail a cab. At least he didn't leave me stranded at the airport.

"Taxi, *por favor*!" yelled Marco. "Taxi, *por favor*!"

"What's he saying?" Katie asked.

"That's Spanish for 'Taxi, please,'" I said. "Don't you know anything?"

"Well, *of course* I knew that. I was just testing you!"

I knew Katie was fibbing. She'd probably been asleep during that lesson at school. I wondered if she could count to ten—even in English.

After a short ride in the taxi, we all got into a boat and sailed up a winding river. Dad was right—this place was nothing like Greenville! I overheard Marco pronounce the name of the river for everyone. Everyone except me, that is. He kept his back to me the entire time.

"Welcome to my home. It's called *Tor-tu-ger-o,*

and it's named after the sea turtles. *Tortuga* is Spanish for 'turtle,'" Marco explained. "They lay eggs on the beaches at night that then hatch and go back into the ocean."

"Amazing!" Dad said.

"*Asombroso!*" Marco said. "That means 'amazing' in Spanish!"

As we sailed up the river, I quickly noticed something moving in the trees: monkeys! They were so cute and looked just like the ones on the animal channel. They were everywhere, swinging by their tails and making little screechy sounds.

Teeny got a little scared.

"It's okay, Teeny," said Marco, patting his head. "The spider monkeys are just curious to see us. But be careful—sometimes they like to play tricks and steal things!"

I checked to make sure that my pencil was still in my ponytail. Suddenly, I looked above my head to see a colorful bird land in the top of a tree. It looked just like Toucan Sam on the Froot Loops box!

"Is that what I think it is?" asked Katie, looking through her binoculars.

"Yes, that is a toucan! We have several different species here in Costa Rica," said Marco, proudly. "Of course, the quetzal is the most beautiful bird, but we hardly ever see any. Some people search their entire lives and never see a single one."

There goes Marco and his crazy imagination again. I wonder if his parents know he likes to make up things.

"Oh, and we have *thousands* of unique plants as well. Some are even used to make medicine!" Marco said. "It's like having a living pharmacy in the backyard."

I couldn't help but roll my eyes and whisper to Katie, "Sure it is; sure it is." I knew better than to believe the whole "living pharmacy" thing. Marco's stories were getting weirder by the minute. Unfortunately, I looked over and noticed him staring straight over at my sister and me. *He is giving me the meanest look ever.*

I quickly tried to ignore him and find my sketch-book. The birds wouldn't sit still long enough for me to draw them. Luckily, Mom brought along a camera.

Marco introduced everyone to his aunt Maria, his uncle Felipe, and his cousin Tica. She looked about the same age as Marco and me.

"Welcome to Costa Rica, O'Banning family!" said Tica's mom. "We're glad to have you visit our beautiful country. We've heard lots about you."

"Are you really an artist?" Tica asked me. "I like art stuff too."

"Awesome!" I said, wondering what else Marco had told her. "I like to draw with colored pencils."

"I paint with watercolors," said Tica. "Maybe I'll show you some of my paintings later."

At least I could get along with *someone* in Marco's family.

"Tomorrow we'll explore further," said Felipe. "Who knows? We may get to do something that you've never, *ever* done before!"

"Yippee!" said Nana. "My crazy pig and I are more than ready!"

Later that night, I was too excited to sleep, and I could hear the animals howling in the jungle. But there was one thing that kept bugging me: *What on earth was Felipe talking about?*

Weird. Very weird.

8

Birds of a Feather

Grr . . . gloop . . . grrp. My stomach was going crazy. Even though we saw lots of cool stuff in the rainforest, I didn't see anything that looked tasty.

"Isn't it time for lunch? I'm starving!" I said.

"I second that," said Katie. "I'm so hungry that I could even eat one of those goofy gummy turtles."

After driving a little farther, Marco's uncle finally stopped at a small restaurant.

"I hope the O'Banning girls like burritos," Felipe said. "This place has the best around!"

I *love* burritos, and so does Katie. Maybe she would get extra flaming hot sauce on hers by mistake. Now *that* would be funny.

When we sat down at the table, I noticed something really odd. The restaurant owner had oranges and grapefruit cut in half and hanging by strings outside.

"What's with the oranges on a string?" I asked Tica. "That's the strangest thing ever."

"*You're* the strangest thing ever!" Katie said.

She was back to her old self again. If only a mosquito could have bitten her on the lip.

"These oranges are feeders," Tica said. "Cool, huh?"

"You can say that again! But what kind of animals eat oranges and grapefruit hanging on a string?" asked Katie. "Is it a tiger? If it is, then I'm outta here! Bring my burrito to the jeep!"

Katie was clueless, but so was I.

Suddenly, a green and purple hummingbird zoomed right above my head. It went straight to an orange and then to the grapefruit. Its wings fluttered so fast that I could barely see them move.

Then another hummingbird came . . . and three more after that. They sounded like a swarm of bumblebees.

"Oh my!" said Mom. "They're everywhere! Quick, someone take a photo of these!"

Dad snapped his camera, and I grabbed my sketchbook. It was a good thing that my Pookie Purple was in my ponytail. I drew a tiny green hummingbird with a purple spot under its chin.

"After we finish eating and put our plates in the recycling bin, I have another surprise for everyone," Marco said.

I wasn't used to putting stuff in a recycling bin. *Strange.* Everything about Costa Rica was different. And what could Marco's family be up to this time? I'd already seen plants, monkeys, and tons of birds. *What else could there be?*

"The owner of the restaurant is a friend of ours," said Marco. "He has a very interesting garden out back."

What was so special about a garden? We had those in Greenville. I even helped Nana with hers sometimes.

Just when I was ready to ask Tica about it, my crazy sister squealed and began packing her mouth with ice. She looked like a gerbil.

"*Yeowwww!* My mouth is on fire!" Katie squealed. "What on earth is in that burrito, Marco?" She fanned her mouth with a napkin. "I feel like I just ate the sun!"

I had to turn my head so my sister couldn't see me laughing. She looked like a human stick of dynamite about to explode. Even Marco couldn't help but giggle.

"We use habanero peppers in the sauce on the burrito you ordered," he said. "It's a special type of pepper that is extra hot. However, a glass of milk always cools down spicy food. Would you like me to get you some, Katie?"

"Forget the glass!" she exclaimed. "Bring me the whole cow!"

———

After lunch, I couldn't wait to see what was so different about a garden in Costa Rica. Marco pointed to a small table with tiny glass bottles sitting on top. This garden was already a weird one.

"*Hola!*" said a man filling up the bottles with red water. "Have you come to feed my birds for me?"

"We have," said Marco. "This is Mr. Hernandez, everyone."

"And these are our friends, the O'Bannings," said Tica.

"*Buenas tardes,*" I said.

"Good afternoon to you too!" said Mr. Hernandez, as he handed me one of the red water bottles. "Watch what happens if you sit here and hold the bottle like this."

All of a sudden a hummingbird zoomed in and sat right on my finger! It stuck its long beak into the bottle and drank the red water inside. I looked over at Nana, and one was eating out of her bottle too.

"Wow! Whatever this stuff is, it must be good."

"It's a type of sugar water," said Mr. Hernandez. "And the red color reminds the birds of flowers in the jungle."

"They must have a sweet tooth!" said Katie. "It does look kind of tasty."

"Don't get any ideas," I giggled. "You need to stick with flaming burritos!"

I couldn't help but notice that Marco laughed at my joke.

9

Stinkville

Nana, Teeny, and I sat in the backseat and looked at a map, trying to figure out just where we were going next. Of course, Teeny tried to eat the map a couple of times and crumpled one side of it with his hairy snout.

"Teeny, what in the world is wrong with you?" scolded Nana. "Bad pig, bad pig! Mind your manners, and stick your head out the window, for goodness' sake. Some fresh air will do you good. I can't take you anywhere these days!"

I couldn't help but laugh at Nana and Teeny arguing. It's not like Teeny could actually understand her. I finally gave him a gummy turtle, and that seemed to calm him down a bit.

"How come Costa Rica has such strange names for everything?" I asked. "I can't even pronounce the name of the place we're going to next."

"They're not strange to me," Marco said. "They're Spanish words that we're used to saying."

Me and my big mouth. Marco and I couldn't get along for two seconds.

"If you ask me, I think 'Greenville' sounds odd, especially the name of that street you live on," Marco added.

"Darcy Street," I reminded him. "What's strange about that? I guess it all depends on where you grow up. What's the name of the place we're going to now?"

"You probably can't pronounce it either," Marco smarted back.

Ugh. He drives me bonkers!

"It's called *Ar-e-nal,*" Tica pointed out. "There's a huge lake . . . and a volcano!"

That's when Katie freaked out.

"A volcano?" she asked. "Excuse me, but *why* are we going there? I'd like to live to graduate from high school—not drown in a molten pool of lava!"

"It's okay, Katie," said Tica. "We'll be far away. But it does have orange lava that flows out of it. It looks cool at night—like the mountain is glowing."

"I can't wait to see it!" I chimed in. "Instead of studying about a volcano in Boring Doring's class, we can see the real thing!"

"*Sí,*" said Tica, "I told you Costa Rica is an amazing place!"

"*Sí, muy buena!*" I said. "Very good!"

I thought Marco might be impressed that I was speaking a little Spanish, but he sure didn't act like it. He ignored me almost the entire time.

After driving up and over several mountains, Felipe finally stopped the jeep. I didn't see a volcano or a lake anywhere.

Weird. Very weird.

"Okay, time for everyone to get out again," said Dad. "Grab your binoculars and your plant books. Let's go into the jungle and explore a little!"

I wanted to see the volcano—not more plants in the jungle.

Katie began spraying herself from head to toe with the grossest-smelling bug spray ever. Why was she acting so bonkers over a few little bugs? The huge cloud of spray caused me to choke. Even Teeny was gasping for air.

"Katie! Enough of the spray!" I yelled. "That fog of stink is going to kill us!"

Katie totally ignored me and followed behind

Nana into the rainforest. Something was different about the ferns, plants, and trees around here. They smelled so good and looked nothing like the ones in Greenville. I followed behind Mom and Dad, and they quickly came to a stop beside a large tree with tiny flowers at its base.

"Katie, Nana, the rest of you—come and see this too," said Dad.

We all gathered near the tree and looked at the leaves and bark.

"This is the cinchona tree," said Felipe. "Its bark is used for medicine to treat malaria."

"What's malaria?" I asked. I didn't remember Dad ever mentioning it at home.

"It's a disease that's spread in very warm climates. It's actually spread by mosquitos and can cause people to get really sick. But thanks to the rainforest, we have medicine that helps."

"See, I told you!" squealed Katie. "I knew I'd need more bug spray around here!" My crazy sister put a death grip on her can of spray.

Here comes Stinkville . . .

I tried breathing through my mouth so I wouldn't inhale Katie's fumes.

It seemed strange that something like tree bark could be used in medicine. Marco had told us that living in Costa Rica was like having a living pharmacy in the backyard. I was beginning to think he was telling the truth . . .

Marco walked past me and over to a bunch of pink flowers. *Is he going to pick flowers for me? I hope he doesn't think I want to be his girlfriend.* I saw what it did to Maddy, and I didn't fancy going gaga over a boy 24/7. It looked exhausting!

"Hey, Chan, over here. I want to show you something," Marco said. "These are Madagascar rosy periwinkles. This plant helps fight cancer. Pretty cool, huh?"

"I'll say! Does everything in the rainforest do something amazing?"

"It sure seems that way," he said. "Like my dad always says, everything has a purpose, even plants. It's too bad that they're disappearing."

"What? *Disappearing?*" I asked, confused.

"Yeah. Every year thousands of acres of the rainforest are cut down. Some people want the land for farming or to have land for cattle. They call it deforestation."

"That's crazy! Don't they know how important these plants are?" I asked, shocked.

"I wish that were true, but it's hard to convince everyone."

"Hey, kids, check out this view!" yelled Nana. She'd gone up ahead and had hiked a little farther.

Then we saw it: Arenal Volcano. Although it was far away, it still looked huge and oozed with lava. I couldn't imagine how hot it was up there. It could probably cook an egg in two seconds!

"Isn't that one of the most beautiful things you've ever seen?" asked Nana.

Marco and Tica were right. It looked like the mountain was glowing.

Even Katie was speechless.

10

Oh, Why Did I Do That?

"Oh, Channn . . . Katieeee . . . up and at 'em, you two!" Nana said. "It's time to get up! The birds are waiting!"

I rolled over and looked at the clock: *6:00 a.m.?*

Great gorillas! Why did we have to get up so early?

Katie's snoring had been loud enough to wake up every monkey in the jungle. I hadn't slept a wink.

"Nana, do you know what time it is?" I asked. "I thought we were on vacation."

I buried my head under my pillow, but Nana ignored my whining. She even sent Teeny in after us. He pranced in, grabbed my blanket, and pulled it off the bed with one jerk. I guess he was ready to go too.

"Okay, okay, you hyper pig! I'm up!"

Katie still hadn't moved a muscle, and Teeny knew it. He quietly walked over and licked her across the mouth.

"*Yuck*! Gross, Teeny! The last thing I need around here is pig slobber!"

After throwing on some clothes, I quickly stuck my Blue Morpho pencil into my ponytail and laced up my zebra-striped sneakers. I grabbed my sketchbook, put the binoculars around my neck, and headed toward the jeep. I felt like a real jungle explorer.

Katie, on the other hand, was more interested in covering every inch of her body with more bug spray. My sister was out of control.

"Have you seen the *size* of the mosquitos around here?" she asked. "They're big enough to carry Teeny away! Everyone better use this stuff!"

Marco and his uncle were already awake too. Tica was helping them put stuff into the jeep.

"Hey, Marco," I said, trying to be nice, "does your family get up early like this all the time?"

"It's best to go bird-watching early since they're

more active in the morning. But I forgot, Channing O'Banning, you don't believe anything that I say!"

Marco stomped off toward the jeep. I guess I deserved it. I'd made fun of Spanish words, laughed at him in front of Katie, and rolled my eyes about a few things he'd said about the rainforest. *But why shouldn't I?* Marco knew a lot about Costa Rica, but that didn't make up for his dumb stories about creepy frogs and birds that have ferns for tails. And he hadn't been very nice to me either—making fun of my grade and looking down his nose at my art.

Sheesh!

"Okay, gang, we're off to the cloud forest!" yelled Dad.

I was totally confused. "Why is the place we're going to called the 'cloud forest'?"

"That's a very good question, Channing O'Banning," said Marco's aunt Maria. "It's very misty and really damp up there—sort of like being in the clouds. Tons of animals like to live in that environment."

"What *kind* of other animals?" asked Katie, turning pale as a ghost. "Anything d-d-d-dangerous?"

"There are all kinds of bats, sloths, and howler monkeys. And if we're lucky, we might even see a jaguar!" Marco said.

"Uh . . . I . . . I think I'll just stay in the jeep!" said Katie.

My sister didn't look so well. Her face had started to turn kind of green.

"There's even an animal called a peccary," said Marco. "It looks like a cross between a pig and a giant hamster."

"*Fantástico!*" giggled Nana. "Teeny, you may find your long-lost cousin!"

After riding in the jeep for awhile, we hiked up a huge mountain. My legs felt like limp noodles, and everything became so damp that my shirt stuck to my skin and my hair felt glued to my head. This had to be the cloud forest!

"Time to get your binoculars!" said Maria. "Here's a photo of a quetzal. Keep an eye out; we may get lucky today. They're almost impossible to find."

Wait a minute . . .

"A *quetzal*?" I asked, shocked at what I'd just heard. "That's a *real* bird?" I looked closer at the photo. "Wow, it looks like it's been painted with a paintbrush!"

"See, I told you!" Marco said, yelling back at me. He was already ten steps ahead and looking into the trees with his binoculars.

If only I could spot a quetzal first! That would show Mr. Jungle Expert.

I remembered Boring Doring telling us that the top of the jungle was called the canopy. We looked everywhere for the quetzal. Each time Mom thought she'd spotted one in the canopy, it was a green fern instead.

"*Psst* . . . Channing, come quick," whispered Nana, up ahead of me. "But be very, very quiet."

Oh, man, maybe Nana had found a quetzal!

I double-checked my ponytail to make sure that I had my pencil. When I got closer, I saw a huge bright-yellow butterfly. Greenville had butterflies, but nothing like this.

"It's called a yellow swallowtail, Chan. Isn't it stunning?" said Nana.

She tiptoed over quickly and took a photo. But I was determined to draw the butterfly while it sat on a flower. Just when I was about to get closer, it flew to another flower . . . and then another . . . and then another. If I could just keep up with it for a few more seconds, I'd have a great drawing.

But then something horrible happened.

I looked up . . . and everyone was gone.

I had followed the swallowtail so far into the jungle that I had gotten away from the others. All of the paths and tree branches started to look alike.

I was lost in the cloud forest!

Marco probably hoped I'd stay lost forever. I yelled for Nana . . . for Dad . . . for Tica . . . even for Katie and Marco.

No one answered.

11

Is That What I Think It Is?

Every tree looked the same, and I was starting to panic. What if I were walking in circles? What if I never got out of the cloud forest? What if a spider monkey stole all of my colored pencils?

Maybe my dingy sister is right. What if some alien-looking insect were lurking in the trees? What if it loved to bite kids with freckles? What if it attacked and then got its legs tangled up in my ponytail? This could be bad. This could be really, *really* bad.

I didn't know where to turn and decided to sit down on a rock and think. Mom always told me that if I ever had a tough choice to make, I should stop and really think about it slowly. I doubt she was talking about getting lost in the rainforest of Costa Rica, but what choice did I have?

Suddenly I heard something. *Chirrrrp . . . chirpppp . . .*

It sounded like a cricket or a frog. Maybe it was a *monster* frog that would eat me—just like the one in my nightmare! My knees began knocking as I saw something jump high out of a plant. At least it looked tiny.

I tiptoed over to get a closer look. I blinked my eyes to make sure I wasn't seeing things.

It was a frog, but it wasn't just your normal, plain ol' frog. Its body was the brightest red I'd ever seen, and its legs were the color of . . . *blue jeans*!

It's a blue jeans frog! Great gorillas! Marco was telling the truth!

Ugh, did I feel dumb! Now I *really* had to tell Marco I was sorry. I couldn't believe that I was staring at an actual blue jeans frog. I quickly got out my sketch-book and drew it before it jumped away.

"Oh, Channnnn . . . Channing O'Banningggggg . . . Can you hear me?"

Wait a minute . . . *I think I hear someone . . .*

"Channn, are you over there? Give us some kind of signal!"

It sounded like Marco!

"Over here! Over here!" I yelled. I couldn't believe it!

In just a few seconds, I suddenly saw Marco coming down the path toward me.

I was rescued! They found me!

But really it was just *Marco* who had found me.

Following behind him was the rest of the gang smiling from ear to ear. *Whew!* I had thought I'd never see them again!

"Thank goodness Marco found you!" Mom cried. "Luckily, he knows the jungle better than any of us. Don't you ever scare us like that again! I thought I'd lost my little artist."

"Yeah, you goofy kid," said Katie. "Next time, take a compass."

As we made our way back to the jeep, I stayed close to Mom and walked beside Marco.

"Uh, Marco, thanks for finding me," I said. "I thought I might have to live in the cloud forest forever and be forced to eat plants and bugs for the rest of my life. And besides that, I owe you an apology. I messed up big time."

Marco was speechless. I think he was in shock.

"I should have believed you at school," I admitted. "While I was lost in the jungle, I actually saw a blue jeans frog. I almost didn't believe it, but I saw it with my very own eyes!"

"See, I told you, Chan! Aren't they cool looking?" asked Marco, smiling from ear to ear.

"Totally cool looking!" I agreed. "And, Marco, you know *lots* more about plants and animals than I ever will. Maybe next year you can help me in science class. It's not one of my best subjects."

"Sure, Chan, no problem," Marco said and then gave me a fist bump. "But only if you can show me how you draw animals so well. I'm not as good at that. Hey, we've got one more thing to do before we leave the cloud forest—zip line!"

Marco ran ahead. I couldn't remember what my dad had explained about zip lining, but I knew now to trust my friend. Everyone was given a helmet to wear and a harness to strap around his or her waist. Even Nana and Teeny wore one.

Judging by the tangled mess of wires, I could tell this was gonna be tricky.

Marco went first and hooked his harness to a

long rope that went from one tree all the way over to another. It was far, far away.

With one jump and a loud scream, Marco zoomed across the top of the jungle, stopping way over on the other side. It looked just like he was flying through the trees! Tica went next, and she flew faster than Marco.

"Yippee! Teeny and I want to go next!" I yelled, getting in line. "Hold on tight, you wild and crazy pig!"

With one big push, Teeny and I flew across the zip line and squealed at the top of our lungs. It was *awesome*! Zip lining was the most fun I'd ever had on any summer vacation! Katie was the last one to come across, and she closed her eyes the entire way.

Just as Marco and I were taking off our helmets, Marco froze in his tracks.

What's wrong with him? Is he sick?

"Shhhh. Quiet everyone," he whispered.

Marco grabbed his binoculars and looked up into the canopy. I quickly copied Marco and looked up into the trees.

"What is it, Marco? Is it . . . a *quetzal*?" I whispered, trying not to scream.

"Hold on. I think . . . I think . . . it is! You're right, Channing!" said Marco. Everyone hurried to look through binoculars.

And there, high up in the canopy, was the

prettiest bird—maybe even the prettiest animal—I had ever seen with my own two eyes. I had never imagined seeing something so vibrantly green—it looked like a fuzzy emerald with wings.

"It's more beautiful than I ever imagined. Look at the shades of green . . . and red . . . and yellow," said Nana. "What an amazing creature!"

"*Asombroso!*" Marco and I said at the same time. We couldn't help but giggle at having the very same thought. It shouldn't have been *that* surprising—good friends think alike lots of times!

12

Time to Fly

It was our last day in Costa Rica, and I didn't want to go home. Even Katie wanted to stay longer. I had no idea that Costa Rica would be such a fun place to visit.

"We have one more surprise before heading to the airport," said Marco.

"Come on, give us a hint," I said.

"Yeah, Marco, just a tiny one," said Katie.

"Okay, okay. Our last stop is a farm, and that's all I'm going to say."

A farm? That's our last stop in Costa Rica?

"What do they grow there? I hope they grow mangos like we ate yesterday. Those things were *delish*!" said Katie.

"Sorry," said Marco. "I don't think so. You'll just have to wait and see."

"Are we going to a coffee plantation, Marco?" I asked. "I read that Costa Rica grows lots of coffee. I think coffee tastes like liquid dirt, but Mom lives on the stuff."

"Wrong again. Sorry, Chan. But we're almost there, so you won't have to keep guessing!"

As we pulled into the driveway of the farm, I noticed there wasn't a barn, or animals, or anything. The only thing that I saw was a large greenhouse.

"Are we at a flower farm, Marco? Is that it?"

"You're getting closer," he hinted. "Something like that."

"Well, let's quit playing guessing games, you silly kids!" said Nana. "Come on, Teeny, let's find out what this last stop is all about. We'll beat them to it."

Nana had only been inside a few minutes when she came running out to find me. Teeny ran back to the jeep faster than a cheetah. He began poking me with his snout like it was some kind of emergency.

"Calm down, you silly pig!" I said, laughing. "What is wrong with you? Have you been drinking Mom's coffee?"

"Channing O'Banning! You'll never guess what's inside that greenhouse!" Nana said, jumping up and down. "You'll want to get that pencil I bought you for the trip. Hurry now, stick it into your ponytail!"

Nana wasn't making any sense, but I did as she asked. I stuck my Blue Morpho pencil into my ponytail and made sure that my sketchbook was in my backpack. The front door was marked with the words Blue Morpho Farm.

Wait a minute.

"Why don't you open the door and go inside?" said Marco.

Teeny pushed me forward with his snout, and I looked up at the ceiling. I could hardly believe my eyes.

It was a butterfly farm!

"Wow!" said Katie. "This is incredible! I've never

seen so many butterflies in my entire life! They're everywhere!"

Katie was right. It was a sea of blue fluttering wings.

"I told you it was a farm! Just different," said Marco. "Costa Rica has more than three thousand species of butterflies."

"Hi, everyone! My name is Mr. Albarez, and welcome to the Blue Morpho butterfly farm! Can you see why the blue morpho is called the most beautiful butterfly on earth? We have them in all stages to help you understand their development."

I quickly grabbed my Blue Morpho pencil from my ponytail and drew what was in front of me.

Teeny went crazy trying to chase the butterflies. One even landed on his tail!

"Here is the butterfly in the caterpillar stage. We try to protect them so they aren't eaten by birds."

Mr. Albarez pointed to several plump, little worms hanging onto plant leaves. They didn't look anything like butterflies.

"These caterpillars will eat, turn white, and go through a molting stage," he said. "Then, at eleven weeks, each one hangs upside down and turns into a chrysalis."

I had no idea that becoming a butterfly was so much work.

"And in just two weeks, the blue morpho appears like magic," said Marco. "Isn't it strange how they go through all of those stages?"

Their wings were the prettiest blue I'd ever seen, like the deepest, clearest blue sky. They almost glowed.

"I guess we all change in our own way," said Nana.

My grandmother was *sooo* right. Just last week I had been mad at Marco over the silliest thing and didn't like him very much. Now he was a great friend, and I couldn't wait to hang out with Maddy, Cooper, and him at school. I guess I needed to stop and really think before making judgments about people—*especially when I didn't know the whole story.*

"I've always heard that if a butterfly lands on you, it means that you're beautiful. I sure hope one lands on me!" squealed Nana.

Within minutes, the butterflies had landed on all of us. Teeny was covered in butterflies from snout to tail! He smiled from ear to ear when Nana took his picture. I couldn't wait to go to the gift shop.

Dad bought me a cool T-shirt with a blue morpho on the back. When I tried it on, it looked just like I had wings. I even bought one for Maddy. She liked butterflies as much as I did.

13

Going Green?

When we finally made it to the airport, I felt sort of sad. Still, I could hardly wait to tell Maddy and Cooper about everything—especially the blue jeans frog. It was a good thing that I had drawn it in my sketchbook.

I could tell it was tough for Marco to say good-bye

too. Greenville was far away, and I'm sure he wondered when he'd be back to see his family.

"It's okay, Marco," I said, trying to make him feel better. "I'm sure you'll come back again. Maybe your family can fly to Greenville one of these days."

Tica overheard us talking and couldn't help but join in.

"*Sí, sí,* Channing O'Banning. I would love to visit America! Maybe my father will let me come and stay with Marco during vacation."

Tica handed me a small present wrapped in a banana leaf and tied with a ribbon.

"It's a small gift to say thank you for visiting my country."

I untied the ribbon to find two new colored pencils! One was called Rainforest Green and the other was Periwinkle Pink. I stuck both of them into my ponytail.

"Now you can draw the rainforest anytime you like!" said Tica. "Make sure to tell your friends about our beautiful jungle. Of course, you can leave out the getting lost part!"

"*Sí, sí!*" I yelled back. "I'll tell them, Tica. *Gracias!*"

After taking our seats on the plane, I got out my sketchbook and tried out my new pencils. I drew a picture of Tica and Marco zip lining through the rainforest. I was going to make doubly sure that my friends in Greenville knew why the rainforest was so important. Marco even said he'd help me.

Teeny cuddled under a blanket and snored louder than Katie. Nana had her head buried in a book called *Going Green Made Easy*.

"That sure is a weird title," I said. "What's it about?"

"It's all about how to go green. Visiting Costa Rica made me realize how important it really is."

Going green? What does that mean?

I wasn't sure what Nana was talking about.

Weird. Very weird.

"Sorry, Nana, but I don't understand," I admitted. "When I didn't put on enough sunscreen at the beach, I turned really pink. But I've never heard of anyone turning green."

Nana smiled and turned to one of the pages in her book.

"Going green means doing any little thing you can to help protect the environment. Don't you think it's important to keep our earth as healthy as possible?"

"Sure, Nana," I admitted. "But I wouldn't even know where to start."

"Well, this book says that every little thing counts. Recycling is an easy way to start. We can recycle plastic, paper, and even glass," Nana continued.

"Makes sense to me!" I said. "Marco mentioned that people are cutting down trees in the rainforest in order to have more land to build things like cities and stuff. Don't they realize that they're destroying animals' homes—*and* destroying medicine that we need?"

"I wish that they did," said Nana. "We need to protect our animals *and* our rainforests."

Nana was right. Maybe I'd go green too.

"What else can we do at home besides recycling?" I asked, looking into her book.

"All sorts of things! We can try to save water at home. Do you keep the water running while you're brushing your teeth?"

"I do keep it running. I don't even think about it," I said, feeling bad. "That's wasting water, huh?"

"I'm afraid so. And do you turn off the lights upstairs when you leave the Secret Artist Hangout?"

Again, I had to tell her the truth. *Gulp.*

"No, sorry, Nana," I admitted. "I guess I'm not very green, huh?"

"Not very green *yet*," she said. "But we can change that when we get back home. Sound good?"

"Sounds *asombroso*! That's 'amazing,' in Spanish, remember?"

"What's amazing is that Marco helped rescue you in the rainforest, and now you can help rescue the rainforest with Marco," said Nana. "Like you always say, Channing O'Banning, that's weird. Very weird!"

14

Green in Greenville

It felt good to be back at my house on Darcy Street. Katie was glad to be home too, since she didn't have to coat herself in bug spray anymore. As soon as we carried our suitcases inside, I asked Mom if I could invite Maddy and Cooper over.

"Sure, Chan," Mom said. "It's good to know that you and Maddy have made up. You two have been best friends for a long time."

"Well, we sorta haven't made up yet. I thought inviting her over might be a good start. After all, I need to give her the gift I bought her," I said. "I thought a lot about our argument at school. I think I overreacted a little."

"I'm so proud that you can admit that, Channing," Mom said, smiling while she hugged my shoulders. "I do believe my little artist is growing up."

If only my plan could work . . .

"Finally, you're back home!" said Maddy, running up the stairs. "That was the longest seven days ever!"

Maddy actually seemed glad to see me!

"Yeah, Greenville was totally boring without you here, Channing O'Banning!" Cooper said. "I got so bored that I even read about the rainforest on the computer. From what I read on those websites, you're lucky you made it back in one piece."

"Sure, I'm fine, silly. Costa Rica is the coolest place *in the world*! There were all sorts of beautiful frogs, birds, and insects," I said. "Oh, and Marco wasn't too bad, either."

Maddy looked at me as if I were an alien.

"*You* got along with *Marco*? And now you think that a frog is beautiful? Did you leave your brain in the jungle?" Maddy asked.

Now was my chance.

"Maddy, can I talk to you in private?" I asked. "Coop, can you give us a few minutes?"

"Girls!" said Cooper. "I just don't understand

your kind. I'll be in the kitchen having a cookie. Something I understand!"

I could feel my heart beating in my chest, and my hands were all sticky.

"Maddy, I think I owe you an apology. I didn't act very nicely to you or Marco at school, and that's my bad. I shouldn't have made you choose between the two of us. That was sorta dumb."

"I forgive you, Chan," Maddy said. "But I shouldn't have gone on and on about how smart Marco is, when I know you struggle in science a little. I should have thought about your feelings a little more. I hope you'll forgive me too."

"So, can we be BFFs again?" I just had to ask.

"Duh!" said Maddy. "That's a no-brainer! Of course we can!"

What a relief to have Maddy back as my forever friend. It was an answer to prayers.

"Are you two finished?" whispered Cooper, peeking into the living room. "I'm getting kinda bored talking to your mom in the kitchen."

"You're crazy, Coop," Maddy and I said at the same time. I shouldn't have been surprised. Best friends think alike lots of times!

I decided to get out my sketchbook and show them some of my drawings. Maddy loved the drawing of the swallowtail I had drawn for her. Of course, I didn't tell her what I had to go through in order to complete it.

We also got on the computer and looked at Dad's photos.

"Wow, these are awesome, Chan!" said Maddy. "You need to bring these to class when school starts back. Boring Doring might even put them on the bulletin board for his students next year."

Did Maddy have to remind me about school? I'd tried blocking Boring Doring out of my head for the summer. But after visiting Costa Rica, I could see why he went cuckoo over plants.

"That's a cool T-shirt you're wearing," said Cooper, "but that is one weird-looking butterfly on the back."

"I think it's beautiful," said Maddy. "Are they really that blue?"

"No," I smiled. "They're even bluer! They're called blue morpho butterflies, just like my colored pencil, and I brought you both back a souvenir."

When I handed Maddy a shirt just like mine, she squealed and even hugged me. It was definitely a BFF kind of hug.

"This is my new favorite shirt, Channing O'Banning! Let's wear them on the first day of school. We'll be twins!"

I handed Cooper a small can with a lid on top. Inside was a plant with a fat green caterpillar. Cooper looked confused.

"Uh, thanks, Chan . . . *I guess.*" Cooper looked down into the can and crinkled his nose. "But what am I supposed to do with a . . . a . . . *worm?*"

Cooper didn't understand—yet!

"This is only the first stage, but in a few weeks it will turn into a beautiful blue morpho butterfly!"

"No way!" said Cooper.

"You mean a real, live butterfly will be in there?" asked Maddy, looking into the can.

"Just make sure it has food. It should change in a few weeks!"

I told them about the butterfly farm and zip lining through the jungle. Cooper really liked hearing about the plants that treat diseases.

"The only things we have in our backyard are weeds," said Cooper. "I doubt if they do anything except make me sneeze."

"The only plant that I know about is poison ivy," Maddy said. "But maybe there's a plant in the rainforest that makes it quit itching like crazy!"

"Probably so," I said, "but the rainforest is disappearing, and that's a big problem! If there's no more rainforest, not only will there be fewer medicines, but no chocolate, bananas, or even chewing gum will exist! All those ingredients come from the rainforest."

Maddy's mouth dropped open, and Cooper looked like he'd seen a ghost.

"And if plants aren't there to trap water into the soil, then the water won't evaporate into the sky and come back down as rain for rivers and streams. Tons of animals and insects will die, not to mention our drinking water will be totally gross. This is serious—big time."

"You've got that right!" said Maddy. "What can we do to stop this?"

"Nana says we need to go green," I pointed out.

"Huh? *Green?*" asked Cooper. "You're back to acting all goofy again, Channing."

"Ta-da!" I said, flipping open my sketchbook. "May I present the amazing list of How to Go Green?"

Maddy and Cooper looked at me like I had three heads. They were clueless . . . *but that was about to change!*

15

Paper or Plastic?

"Okay, let's hear it," sighed Cooper. "But sometimes, Channing O'Banning, your plans are a little . . . well . . . *out there*."

"Yeah, and sometimes they end up being a major disaster!" Maddy said. "Remember the Greenville pet show? We had animals running all over the school! I even got fleas!"

"Shhh! Don't even mention that," said Cooper. "You'll make me feel creepy-crawly all over again. I still have nightmares about that kid in second grade with the pet rat. Why would anyone want such a thing?"

"Going green means doing stuff every day to save water or electricity," I said. "It keeps our earth clean."

"Oh, so that's it!" said Cooper. "I think my dad is going green at my house. He has our trash divided up in the kitchen. He has one bag for paper and one for plastic. At first, I thought he was practicing to be a garbage man!"

"He's being smart and recycling," I said. "If your dad takes the stuff to a recycling center, it can be made into something else. Otherwise, it ends up in a big, Stinkville trash landfill."

"Land filled with trash? Now *that's* totally gross!" said Maddy. "What else can we do to be green?"

"You can turn off the lights when you're not using them," I said. "And you could walk to school or ride with us instead of having your mom drive her car."

"That sounds simple enough," said Maddy.

"Hey, my dad said something like that too. If we reduce the number of cars, then there will be less harmful and smelly junk in the air," Cooper added.

Maddy was deep in thought about what I'd just said.

"Are you sure you didn't hit your head on one of those banana trees? You're not the same, Channing O'Banning."

"Sure I am, Maddy," I said. "I'm just a little smarter, thanks to Marco and Costa Rica. We need to talk about my plan to save the rainforest too. I've got lots of cool ideas about how to stop deforestation. Nana, Marco, and I talked about it on the plane. Oh, and did you know that Marco is a genius when it comes to plants?"

Maddy and Cooper looked at each other and rolled their eyes.

"It's just too weird. When you left for vacation, you couldn't stand Marco!" Cooper said. "If only that crazy pig of your Nana's could talk. Maybe he could explain what's happened to you."

"Let's just say I was a little lost," I admitted. "Marco's pretty cool when you get to know him. He's even going to help us with a 'Go Green in Greenville' plan when school starts back. Will you help us?"

"We're best friends, aren't we?" asked Maddy. "But please, no fleas this time!"

"Count me in too," said Cooper, smiling. "Because I have a feeling you'll make me help anyway."

Cooper was right. Maybe he'd even blab and tell the whole school about it.

This time, I wouldn't mind at all.

THE END

Did You Know?

1. Half of the world's plant and animal species live in the tropical rainforests of the world.
2. Thirty acres of trees are cut in tropical rainforests *every minute*. Every second, a portion of rainforests the size of a football field is destroyed. This is called *deforestation*. When this happens, many animal species could become extinct.
3. The rainforests are a potential source of medicinal plants that can benefit every single person on earth.
4. Items such as coffee, gum, chocolate, cinnamon, perfume, tires, and rope are all made from plants that can only grow in the rainforests.
5. We need the rainforests to produce oxygen and clean the atmosphere to help us breathe.

Want to Save the Rainforests? Here's How!

1. Tell your friends! Just like Channing O'Banning, organize a "Go Green!" activity at your school. Set up recycling bins: one for paper and one for plastic. Make sure your friends and teachers use them. This will help make the earth greener, healthier, and cleaner!

2. Many animals from the rainforests are brought to our country illegally. Parrots and iguanas, for example, are often imported illegally. Do not buy these animals, since that encourages other people to bring more animals.

3. Have a bake sale or school fund-raiser to raise

money to donate to an organization that works to conserve rainforests.

4. Read about other children who live in and near rainforests; see how they and their families depend on the plants and animals in rainforests.

5. Ask your teacher to teach your class more about rainforests.

6. Do a class project to learn more about rainforests and the plants and animals that live there. Create a skit, write a story, or decorate your classroom to look like a real rainforest!

7. Write a letter to an organization or company that is working to protect the rainforest and tell them they're doing a great job!

8. Look at a map of the world with your parents or teacher, and point out the places where rainforests exist.

9. Look around your home for things you use or eat that originate in the rainforests; think about how many things we use every day that originate in the rainforests and how it would affect you if they were no longer around.

www.rainforest-alliance.org

Want to learn more about Channing O'Banning? Find out where the famous fourth grade artist is going next! Check out www.channingobanning.com.

Check out the second book
from Channing O'Banning.

1

Dig In!

"There it is! There it is!" said my best friend, Maddy. She used a paintbrush to sweep away the dirt and get a closer look.

"Are you *sure* we're supposed to use a paintbrush for this?" I asked. "This is weird, Maddy. Very weird."

I wondered if my best friend knew what she was

doing. After all, *I'm* the expert when it comes to using art stuff.

"Oh, but it's *not* weird to keep a pencil stuck in that ponytail of yours?" Maddy asked. "I wouldn't talk about weird if I were you, Channing O'Banning!"

Maddy did have a point. But I liked to be ready to draw at all times. Having a pencil in my ponytail made perfect sense to me.

"As for my paintbrush, this is how they do it on *Quest for Bones*. I'm positive," Maddy continued.

"She's right," Cooper interrupted. "They use all kinds of different brushes to sweep away dirt. Once, they uncovered a fossil that was actually a dinosaur egg?

Cooper always explained every single thing he'd seen on *Quest for Bones*. He told us whether we asked about it or not.

"Hmmm . . ." Coop said, pushing his glasses back up on his nose, "I wonder if cavemen ate dinosaur eggs for breakfast? That would be one big omelet!"

Maddy and I stared at Cooper like he was an alien. Sometimes his brain was on another planet. *Who cares if cavemen ate omelets?*

We got down on our hands and knees and looked closer at the rocks. We'd been digging in the same exact spot for a whole week. On days when it was too cold to go outside, we stayed in at recess and planned our next move.

The whole thing started when Cooper dared me to race him to the end of the playground. Of course, I would have easily beaten him by a mile if I hadn't tripped over a dumb rock. I even tore a hole in my zebra high-top sneaker. It was *totally* embarrassing. Not only did I trip on a rock and wreck my favorite shoes, but I let a boy beat me in an easy race. That was just plain wrong.

But the rock that tripped me didn't look like any normal rock. It was gray in some spots and white in other places. Part of it was sharp and part of it was smooth.

So Maddy and Cooper decided to start digging and digging and digging. Did I mention there was digging? Because there was—*every single day.* Cooper and Maddy were sure there was something amazing buried under the Greenville Elementary playground, but I didn't really care. I just wanted my friends to get more interesting hobbies, *ASAP!*

We'd even been studying about rocks in Mr. Doring's science class. Boring Doring gave each one a fancy long name that I could barely pronounce. *Why can't rocks have non-weird, easy-to-remember names?*

"Got any other ideas of what it might be, Maddy?" Coop asked anxiously. He had rocks on the brain.

"I'm not sure, Coop," Maddy answered and continued to brush away dirt. "I wonder if it's some sort of fossil."

"Really?" Cooper squealed. "That would be so cool. Maybe there are arrowheads under there too! Dig harder, Maddy! Dig harder!"

"Move out of the way, Cooper, and let me get a better look," I insisted.

"Don't be so bossy, Channing O'Banning. If it weren't for me daring you to a race, or should I say *beating* you in a race, we wouldn't have made this discovery in the first place."

"Don't remind me," I mumbled. "I wish I'd never agreed to your crazy challenge. I could have saved myself a shoe! Come on, let's go do something else."

Anything has to be better than this. Even playing on the monkey bars. My palms get sweaty and I usually end up falling off before I'm even halfway across. But even *that* is better than digging in the same boring spot for all eternity.

"Hey, Chan," Maddy suddenly asked, "will you do a sketch of the rock for us? You never know, we might need it later."

Yes! Finally, something I like to do. Scratch that—something I love to do!

I looked closer at the dig site and pulled my Gray Elephant colored pencil from my ponytail. Nana bought it for me when I was into drawing African animals, so that's why I named it Gray Elephant. It was times like this that I was glad to have a pencil close by. Plus, it looked cool in my ponytail. I drew a picture of our dig site in my sketchbook. Drawing was much more interesting than playing around in the dirt, anyway. Before long, I was finished with my sketch.

"Want me to help brush away the dirt, Mad?" I asked. *The sooner we get to the bottom of this, the sooner we can do something else at recess.*

"Sure, Chan, but try not to damage anything. This might end up in a museum or something."

"A museum? That would be awesome!" Cooper screamed at the top of his lungs.

"Shh . . . not so loud!" Maddy whispered. "We don't want the whole school knowing about our discovery yet! Anyway, we have to stop digging and go to social studies class. Bummer."

"Oh, why does that goofy bell ring just when we're getting to the good part?" Cooper whined. "I wish we could wait and have social studies class tomorrow."

I didn't mind going to our next class. Social studies was one of my favorite subjects, besides art, of course. Mr. Reese always made class fun and sometimes even a little crazy. When we studied about ancient Egypt, he came to class dressed up like a mummy (Cooper almost fainted). When we learned about China, Mr. Reese gave everyone a fortune cookie and even showed us how to use chopsticks. No matter how hard I tried, I could *not* get my fingers to hold them the correct way. I almost poked Maddy's eye out just trying to pick up a wad of paper!

This week we were supposed to study Native Americans. It sounded totally boring.

"Don't be such a grouch. Learning about Native Americans might be fun," Cooper said.

"Not to me. You guys are such nerds. I wonder which Indians he'll talk about today. They all seem the same to me—*bor-ing*!"

"Not really, Chan," Cooper said as we walked into class. "They're all really different. And they're called Native Americans—*not* Indians. Don't you remember what Mr. Reese said yesterday?"

I didn't have a clue, but luckily, I could tell Maddy didn't either, which made me feel a teensy bit better. Sometimes my BFF and I get busted for talking in class and not paying attention. Come to think of it, yesterday was one of those days.

"Native Americans lived here long before we did," Cooper pointed out. "The only reason they were called Indians is because Columbus thought he was in India when he landed here."

Now I was really confused, but I didn't dare admit it to Coop. I didn't see why we had to study this sort of stuff.

"Columbus traveled to India?" Maddy asked. "Wow, I had no idea."

"You still don't, silly," Cooper laughed. "Columbus was in North America but *thought* he was in India. He didn't realize he'd blown off course and was way over in America."

Cooper traced the distance from America to India on a map. "Crazy, huh?" he asked.

"Yeah, crazy!" I blurted out without thinking. "I guess you could say that Columbus really lost it!"

Everyone laughed at my joke. Even Mr. Reese giggled a little.

After checking attendance, our teacher had a surprise for everyone. Mr. Reese brought out a small cardboard box from his supply closet and set it on his desk. Maybe we were getting new pencils? Or maybe he'd brought candy for all of us? *maybe* he had gummy turtles for the entire class? Then he'd be my favorite teacher forever!

But Mr. Reese reached inside the box and pulled out three things: a tiny blue rock, a pot with two holes in the top, and a plastic dinosaur. *What is he up to this time?*

Weird. Very weird.